The Sausage Spy

Written by Jill Eggleton
Illustrated by Trevor Pye

Rigby

Sid had a sausage shop.
He made the best sausages
in the world.
People came every day
to Sid's shop.
They left with bags
of his sausages.

3

Mickey Maloney
had a sausage shop, too.
But the people did not like
his sausages.
"Mickey Maloney's sausages
are too little," they said.
"Mickey Maloney's sausages
are too hot!"

Mickey Maloney put on a black hat and black glasses.
"I'm going to be a spy," he said.
"I'll see how Sid makes his sausages.
Then I'll make the best sausages in the world!"

Mickey Maloney sat
in Sid's shop.
He saw how Sid made
his sausages.
"I can make sausages
like that," he said.

Mickey Maloney
went back to his shop.
He made 500 sausages
just like Sid's.
"Now the people will
come to my shop," he said.
"I can make the best
sausages in the world."

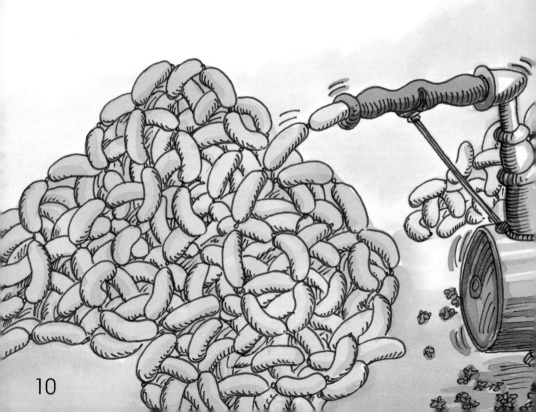

But Sid put a new billboard
by his shop.
It said . . .

Meatballs.
The
best
in the
world
. Sold here.

"Meatballs," said the people.
"We want meatballs.
We have had too many
sausages!"
And they went into Sid's shop
for meatballs.

Mickey Maloney looked
at his 500 sausages.
Then he put a new billboard
by **his** shop.
It said . . .

And Mickey Maloney sold
his sausages to spies!

Billboards

▬▬▬ **Guide Notes**

Title: The Sausage Spy
Stage: Early (3) – Blue

Genre: Fiction
Approach: Guided Reading
Processes: Thinking Critically, Exploring Language, Processing Information
Written and Visual Focus: Billboards

THINKING CRITICALLY
(sample questions)
- What do you think this story could be about?
- What do you know about spies?
- Why do you think the people loved Sid's sausages?
- Look at pages 4 and 5. How do you think the people feel about Mickey Maloney's sausages?
- Look at pages 8 and 9. Why do you think Sid didn't notice Mickey Maloney? What do you think Mickey Maloney will do now?
- Look at pages 12 and 13. What do you notice that is different on this billboard?
- Look at page 14. What do you think is special about Mickey Maloney's sausages now?

EXPLORING LANGUAGE

Terminology
Title, cover, illustrations, author, illustrator

Vocabulary
Interest words: spy, billboard, meatballs
High-frequency words (new): every, black
Compound words: billboard, meatballs

Print Conventions
Capital letter for sentence beginnings and names (**M**ickey **M**aloney, **S**id), periods, exclamation marks, quotation marks, commas, ellipses